LAST DAYS OF POMPEII

by the same author

LAST DAYS OF POMPEII
a comedy
VOLUME 1, AUGURS

Steve Hanson

ERRATUM PRESS

ISBN: 978-1-7397708-2-2

First edition.

This book is a work of fiction. Any resemblance to actual persons, living or dead, are coincidential.

First published in 2022 by Erratum Press
Sheffield, UK
www.erratumpress.com

Design and typesetting by Ansgar Allen

ACKNOWLEDGEMENTS

Thank you to Abby Kearney for a generous but keen early reading
of this—resulting in amendments.

'...ambition, vengeance, unhallowed love, the thirst for warlike renown, and suchlike. The old poets lived in an atmosphere impregnated with these passions, and felt vividly what they expressed...'

1.

Over there was a man who claimed to be a communist.

In the office upstairs was a man who had been promoted over him, who hated the man who claimed to be a communist. The loathing was mutual.

The newly promoted man upstairs claimed to be an anarchist. He wore Black Spot Sneakers. They were the anti-corporate alternative to Nike, who own Converse.

These 'sneakers'—they were American—were made of hemp and recycled tyre soles and were trade union certified.

He had paid the best part of £300 to have them shipped to his stripped-down reclaimed wood flat in Hulme.

He had bought the place just at the right time, getting a mortgage and doing it up in a semi-modernist style.

The man who claimed to be a communist had just bought a place out near Buxton, a 'wreck' he had just about managed to get a mortgage on, with significant financial assistance from his family.

A woman came in. She called people 'old man' and 'old chap' and sounded as if she had stepped out of a time tunnel from the 1940s. Her father had been high up in the navy. She had gone to the Royal College of Art and constantly said so.

'RCA' slithered through her speech, it was a kind of glue, 'arsey eh'. She wore brightly coloured clothes, and thought of herself as an art school bohemian.

The man who claimed to be a communist and the man who claimed to be an anarchist both hated her guts, despite the fact that the man who claimed to be a communist had snogged and groped her in the car park of the pub across the road after the Christmas piss-up in 2014.

The man who claimed to be an anarchist arrived.

Another man came in right behind him wearing Rohan walking trousers and a tweed jacket. Jerry. He looked like a much greyer version of Captain Haddock. Jerry was the painting teacher.

Then Alex, who always said he was a film-maker, although he hadn't completed a film since 1996. Nobody knew this.

What all these people inarguably are is Managers, and today is the Management Meeting. They all knew that because they had all received an email from the PA to the Dean of School which said so.

Everybody hated the PA to the Dean of School. Everybody hated the Dean of School. This united all of them. In fact only this, along with the fact they were all comfortable with lying during interviews, united them.

All of the Management for the Art School clustered around modern coffee urns. Most of them behaved as if they were completely alone in a field, clutching a thermos flask, rather than facing the refreshments table in a scrum, with a serial killer's stare, holding a disposable white coffee cup.

Some of them—mainly those who shared offices—chatted to each other about the summer break.

The man who claimed to be a communist stared at the sneakers of the anarchist from upstairs. He focused his hatred on them. The man who claimed to be a communist wore burgundy Dr Marten's shoes.

The previous term the man who claimed to be an anarchist

had been reported to HR by the local trade union branch for bullying.

But his style of management was a passive psychological warfare and nobody could pin any evidence on him. Even man-who-claimed-to-be-an-anarchist didn't know how he did it. An animal layer of him just under the surface of his skin maintained this fine balance between seething aggression and professionalism.

Several of his staff had briefly contemplated suicide, before leaving.

The man who claimed to be a communist was heavily involved in the trade union. Staff retention figures were to be the next line of attack on the man who claimed to be an anarchist.

Both of them were on the university Ethics Committee, which met once a term.

Behind them, somebody started talking about a paper they had had published, in a louder than necessary voice.

The new realism had been a hot topic the previous term. They all tried to claim they had been in on this first. Of course, it was inevitable that one of them would have been the first to get to it, and one of them had been reading Roy Bhaskar in the 1980s.

But he never mentioned it, and none of the others knew this.

All of them were desperately trying to forget that they had been writing weak papers on Postmodernism up until quite recently.

Some of them had been writing quite a lot of book reviews, to expand the more recent parts of their staff profile, so that it would push the papers on Postmodernism down, away into the past, into amnesia.

Nobody got that far down the list, surely?

'Nobody reads our staff profiles, surely?' the man who claimed to be a communist joked, just a little too loudly, so the exclamation floated in the air above him in a little balloon, before being shot to rubber ribbons by the hate lasers of the assembled staff.

The man who read Roy Bhaskar in the 1980s knew exactly how many people did look at his staff profile, because he once went to the IT staff to find out. It wasn't many, but again, he never mentioned it.

A member of staff had given a talk on a Bruno Latour paper about the Challenger Space Shuttle disaster and 'thick description'. Some of the staff—now they could edit their own profile pages—had given themselves new titles. 'Vital Realist Photographer' for instance, and 'Film-maker exploring the potentiality of thick description'.

The man who read Roy Bhaskar in the 1980s realised that the talk on the Bruno Latour paper was missing the larger philosophical context of Latour's work and as a consequence had made several very telling errors.

Only he had noticed this, but again, he never mentioned it.

He didn't mind the research errors he detected in the work of his colleagues, but he hated the use of meaningless words such as 'potentiality'.

Still, he had applauded with the rest of the staff, all of whom claimed the talk on Bruno Latour was 'brilliant', before slagging it off back in their shared offices, using words such as 'vapid', 'dated' and 'clueless', despite not understanding the larger philosophical context of Latour's work, or noticing the errors in the presentation, and saying things like 'there was too much focus on functionality', as though it actually meant something.

They would turn to their PC's and write narratives in which a snowstorm of itty words began to swirl. Futurity, toxicity. As though these massive signifiers had any chance of connecting to a solid signified, in a tiny abstract essay, in a provincial university. As though the concept of the future had an essence, it did not.

But today was different. The Manager who had been published was now talking about 'the Anthropocene'. Her voice rang out louder and clearer as the rest of the staff went quiet.

It was the scorching silence of the plains before the Cheetah pounces on the Antelope from a high tree.

He reflected on his assumption that the provincial was not geographically confined to the provinces. It could be found in major cities. He reflected further, not for the first time, that this was perhaps the book he really needed to write. But the thought deflated instantly, like a cake that failed to rise. Wouldn't it be better to simply leave and start writing horrible satirical fiction? Better to have the bravery of conviction, rather than engage in this sicked-up discourse, simply because it allowed you to remain in the building. He did not want to remain in the building. He wanted to leave the building.

He finally got to the refreshments table to find it a Somme of shot-down teabags, vegan brownie crumbs and spilled Soy Milk.

But there were no cups. Where all the standard issue white coffee cups were, a series of black orbs now sat, perfectly spaced.

For. Fuck's. Sake.

'Are you coming to the meeting?' the man who claimed to be a communist asked.

'No,' he said.

'I was going to get some coffee, but I best go get set up now.'

'Have you got everything you need?' the man who claimed to be a communist enquired.

'Yeah, be fine,' he replied. The man who claimed to be a communist was his line manager.

He did not want to remain in the building. He left the office. That was a start.

He was an hourly paid lecturer. He couldn't afford coffee and so relied on university catering.

He had no money. He was firefighting around the top end of a two thousand pound overdraft constantly. If he had some overdraft limit left before payday he would buy two bottles of wine, consume both of them over the course of the evening—processing all the bitterness and fury, resolving to do all kinds of radical things—before passing out.

He had set up a Facebook group for casual staff. Some casualised lecturers at the University of Durham had just won concessions as 'the Durham Casuals'.

Inspired by this, he had designed a logo, posted the current problems and asked for any thoughts from the colleagues he had added to the group.

Nobody responded, but a woman whose research focused on protests had taken him to one side and then taken him to task for adding her to the casual staff Facebook group.

She had gone so far as to suggest that his action was 'unethical'. He told her that he had no money and that something needed to be done. She told him of her need 'to get on'.

He cursed his colleagues, that one, the one who is always talking about ethics, and the other one, the guy who is always talking about the politics of representation and then trolling people on Twitter about it.

But he had been a graphic designer and had worked in corporate environments. He had fled those hellholes thinking the public sector would be better, just before the public sector turned private.

Still, at least he had the two grand overdraft limit from the time when he earned real money.

Finally, after holding it off, even though it had hovered millimetres from the core of his being for years, probing him for ways to get in, he was depressed.

He had been getting up, going into work without eating, only noticing he hadn't eaten in the afternoon. He needed to see a doctor.

He got to the lecture theatre and switched the PC on.

He realised that the sound cable had been unplugged straight away.

He had enough experience to expect that the lecture theatre equipment would be in the same state had some maniac with a burning political belief tried to sabotage it for ideological reasons.

He knew that it would be in this state every time he tried to set up, not just occasionally. He knew that this was entirely due to lecturers dismantling and reconnecting things randomly to try to get them working.

Lecturers with PhDs, most with published books and papers, some with awards for their intellectual work.

He managed to check everything over and reconnect the wires that had been unplugged. He pocketed the memory stick left in the USB port.

He would have a nose at the contents later that evening, before handing it to reception the day after.

He bent down to get his own memory stick from his bag, before realising that he had left his bag back in the Management Meeting.

He ran back, sweating. He opened the door a crack. A heated discussion was underway.

…but why close critical theory down…remember that thing that happened last year, in the toilets?…yes, but…well you didn't close the toilet and put the member of staff who cleans the toilet on reception did you?

[There was a pause.]

…where is this going? Because frankly…but that's what you are doing to critical theory.

He felt the silence that came after this last statement physically, a bag of lead in his stomach.

…but…the person who cleans the toilets didn't watch the thing that happened, not report it, and then let it keep happening… true, but… well then what's your problem? This needs to end… there are students trying to finish off PhDs in that department and they don't want a PhD from a dead institute, and you're going to pay out hundreds of thousands to end a thing that has brought in millions…

He slid through the door and into the room, padded as softly as he could to his bag, picked it up, turned and went back to the door.

'Are you alright there?' the man who claimed to be an anarchist asked, with a hint of menace.

'Sorry, forgot my bag,' he said, and left.

When he got back to the lecture theatre someone was there.

A man had logged into the PC he had just set up and opened a PowerPoint presentation. The title screen read The Contemporary Sublime.

'Er, I'm sorry I'm booked in here eleven until one,' he said, walking down the steps towards the front of the lecture theatre, where the man looked up from the screen.

'Who are you?' the man asked indignantly, 'are you part of the department?'

'Which department?' he asked.

'Arts and Humanities.' The man took off his blazer and put it over the chair, a clear territorial challenge.

'Yes I am,' he replied.

'Look, I'm booked in here,' he said, pulling out his iPhone to get the room booking up on screen.

But his iPhone had died. Unable to afford to renew his contract, he had transferred it to a pay-as-you-go supplier two years ago and the battery life was now negligible. If it lasted the morning he was lucky.

He rummaged in his bag and pulled out the charger. He plugged it into the phone and then into the wall.

The man was now going through his slides. 'The Wanderer Above the Sea of Fog' by Caspar David Friedrich.

'Right,' he said, switching the plug on, 'I'm going to phone room booking.'

The man ignored him and brought up another slide. 'Sea of Ice' by Caspar David Friedrich.

As he marched down the corridor his brain burned internally with Tourette's terrorism:

Fucking fuck. Fucking canvas. Fucking cliches. Fucking painting on fucking Friedrich. Fucking total cliche. When will these people learn that some paint on a fucking canvas has not fucking gone beyond beauty and into terror. Or the fucking concept the useless fucking painting...

His brain found more and more ways to insert swear words into other swear words. It operated without his permission these days with frightening, inventive ease. A doctor would call it Ideation.

Which reminded him. He needed to see a doctor.

He burst into the office he had been designated. It was occupied by Vicky, who grudgingly accepted his occasional presence.

'What's the matter,' she said, as he marched in abruptly and picked up the phone.

'Someone in my fucking lecture room,' he said.

'What? Again!' Vicky responded, performing a pained look and rolling her eyeballs around.

He dialled the code for room booking. The dial tone kept shifting in thirty second intervals, indicating that it was ringing around the extensions in an office that was either empty, or in which the phone was being ignored.

He slammed the phone down hard. 'Deep breaths,' Vicky said, darting a glance sideways before returning to her own PowerPoint slides.

'Ruinology' the title screen read, subtitle 'The Contemporary Sublime'.

That did it. Something snapped in him.

He rushed out of the room and down the corridor, turned left and up the next set of stairs, across the bridge and into the second wing of the building—the one which had won an architectural award the year before, despite being impossible to find your way around in—and across the second floor balcony and through the Human Resources suite.

Through the window he could see that a party of some sort was underway.

There were balloons, cake and what looked like champagne, probably prosecco.

He had no time to look properly. His lecture was due to begin in ten minutes.

The cranking of the lift opposite sounded like a prelude to Harkonnen attack.

He burst into room booking to find a young woman in a party hat eating trifle out of a small paper bowl.

'I need a room booking checking,' he said. The repeated 'ings' suddenly sounded indecent, coupled with the sweat on his face.

She put her bowl and plastic spoon down carefully on a paper napkin, stood up and smoothed down her skirt.

'Don't you have access to the App?' she asked, puzzled.

'Quick,' he panted, 'I need it now, my lecture is due to start, someone is in there...'

A subliteral part of him registered the unconscious desires falling out of his mouth like bloody, smashed teeth.

She turned and sat at one of four PC screens in a row.

'What's your staff number?' she asked, calmly.

'Shit,' he said, 'my staff card is in my bag.'

'Don't you remember it?' she asked, 'what's your National Insurance number?'

He told her and she made 'hmm' sounds and clicked leisurely through some screens, asking a series of banal questions about his department, role and level.

He twitched and shifted from foot to foot. Now he needed to pee as well.

Finally she found his timetable. 'Yes,' she said, 'you are booked in G4 from now until 1pm'.

'Can you print it off please?' he asked.

She sighed and right clicked through a few more commands.

The printer chugged and whirred.

'It hasn't printed anything off yet today,' she explained, 'it will probably need to calibrate.'

His entire being drained out through his collapsed shoe soles and seeped into the bristling, heavy duty carpet.

Eventually, with two decisive drones the paper came out. He grabbed it and ran.

As he arrived back at the lecture theatre students were already beginning to fill up the room. Smüg bags on their backs, coats with hoods.

Some of them looked at him with a sly grin.

He ran in clutching his piece of paper, but the man had gone. A single slide hung over the room.

Luc Tuymans, "Within" (2001) Oil on Canvas, 223 x 243cm.

He unplugged the PC from under the desk. The screen went blank. The projector switched to standby. The lecture theatre was nearly full and the students were noisily chatting.

He booted up the PC and plugged in his memory stick.

His iPhone had charged and he could see he had two missed calls from an unknown number.

'Alright everyone, turn off your phones,' he shouted.

4h ago EU data supervisor probes EU bodies' software deals with Microsoft

4h ago Debenhams' fate in the balance after Ashley rescue plan rejected

4h ago Summitry Night Fever—Decoding the Brexit showdown

2.

Len is standing at the bar glowering.

Nine empty barrel glasses stand to the side of his arm like fat, obedient children.

The tenth is being drained slowly.

Uncle Robert is slouching so far down the barstool his weight may pull him off it and on to the floor.

Tod staggers across the dancefloor, waves of emotion, colour and sound flood him, booze, music and disco lights. The sensations wash over in quick succession, mingling with one another.

Drone tone followed by dance beat, green light, red light, happy then sad. The usual Saturday night synaesthesia for an unusually happy funeral party.

Uncle Robert lolled. His opening and drooping eyelids a slow wave goodbye before he crashes forward onto the bar top, one leg hanging like an abandoned swing.

Tod reaches Aunt Marie, stood at the edge of the dancefloor, a plump little island of ruddy-cheeked warmth, and hugs her.

She tells him that the service was nice and the reverend was nice and the spread is lovely. She chews another corner from a daintily quartered chicken sandwich.

'I love you Aunt Marie,' Tod slurs, hugging her ageing body, his massive bulk obliterates her from sight.

The pace quickens, red, orange, green, the disco lights blurring as he sways with Aunt Marie to the music. He closes his eyes but the lights still come through.

He feels his stomach begin to float but realises too late what this means.

He backs off from Aunt Marie and his cheeks fill with warm liquid, red light, green light, he tries to keep it in, his cheeks ballooning, Dizzy Gillespie style, orange light, red light, green... and it's out.

Aunt Marie screams as the vomit just misses her lace-trimmed dress. Tod drops to his knees with a groan, rolls over on to his side and passes out.

3.

A Shock, a painful loud sound. In the first seconds he doesn't know who he is. All he can see is the blue glow as his feed kicks in. The smashed bits of a planet swinging round a white dwarf star. 6:30. For now this is all there is in the universe, three numbers and an Aphex Twin drone.

At 6:32 his identity slowly begins to emerge, along with the full extent of his hangover.

Countrymen, hear me for my cause, be silent so you may hear. Do you believe my honour? I have stolen houseplants, kitchen appliances and books. Most of all books.

Does this make it right? Because I am a poor scholar, employed by this iniquitous assemblage? Censure me in your wisdom, and awake your senses, that you may better judge.

If there be any in this assembly that say my love for the Revolution was no less than his...

Why did I rise against it? Not that I loved it less, but that I loved it more.

Not like Houellebecq. Not like those nihilists on the right of this island.

I must have drawn cocks with hanging balls and something shooting out of the end in the middle of every flipchart in my wing of the building.

Towards the exam board last year I wrote on the blank side of the paper in the photocopier tray. Profane messages. Messages of brutality and unreason.

Yes it was me. And I was at that meeting in which The Dean turned over the agenda to reveal to all the slogan:

I SMELL OF TOOTHPASTE

The myth which arose thereafter claimed nobody present could have done it, as they wouldn't be able to sit to see the result of their action.

Naive, naive.

Had you rather the Long Revolution were living, and die all slaves, than the Long Revolution were dead and live free? It no longer merits the name. It was unambitious, I slew it. The revolution of '68 is dead. Long live The Revolution.

But this is pompous. I did not kill it. We all did. With our amnesia, indolence and ignorance.

Into the office.

Corrugated coffee cup. Paracetamol pill packet. An Ibuprofen box and folded disclaimer in the wastebin. Punch the on button. The circle, slotted at the top like a clocking-in card, glows.

The machine boots up slowly. People scratch, yawn, chat, adjust clothing. Complain about their knees, backs and cartilage damage.

A creeping sense that he was being judged seeped in, without being able to say why.

Just the coincidence of silence. When he talked, others did not. A huge yawn blanked out his hearing leaving a visual fish tank. He held himself like that, enjoying the absurdity of his colleagues' mouths moving silently.

Staff cards hung round their necks bearing photographs of their cadaverous avatars. Their slavery-per-hour faces.

The most narrowly delimited version of themselves, but the version of themselves they were for most of their time. They are this so they can be that other self, smiling back briefly in Mediterranean selfies.

The Email.

It was no great moment. No crossing of the Rubicon. No announcement that the demands from the other side had not been met and so we are at war. It did not describe the shooting of an Archduke, or a president, or the vapourising of a city in the far east. It advised all staff that they were now, fully, legally, service providers, and those people who were once known as 'students' were their customers.

There was no shock as it had been this way for some time. Since the imposition of student fees at least.

But there it was and somehow the Rubicon had been crossed, at the same time as it had already been done, back in what? 2009? 2010?

But here it was. All those rich traditions from Erasmus to Ruskin through to Paulo Freire.

'Education for education's sake' hung in the university gallery on a piece of engraved wood. All messages change with their context and this piece of wood was beginning to look like a clumsy satire.

The gallery. The red brick pillars. The classical form built in the materials of industry and city pride.

The Doric column began as a tree in a clearing hung about with flora and fruit. Then was made permanent in marble. Then here, in this northern region, it was remade through Victorian classicism, in red brick. The branding of the time by Renaissance wannabes with their Mechanics Institutes and 'radicalism'.

As the Corinthian capital mimics the leaf of the acanthus, so the capitals of these columns imitated...

All of it had been cancelled out by The Email. The Consumer Rights Act. But The Email was a fait accompli, it merely enshrined in layman's legal terms a situation that had already come to be.

It was just the confirmation for his part of the world that he had been living for all his life through a morally weak epoch.

In his part of the world the word 'moral' could not be spoken. If it were all buttocks within earshot would clench tight together.

At the same time everyone regularly signed ethics forms which were tick box allegiances to a set of morals which nested the flimsily concealed reality of a legal disclaimer for the institution, the university.

Answering the question with a pre-supposed answer in order to then be approved was a moral process. They were morals forms.

Nobody could think anymore.

Well, a few people still could and Raymond was one of them.

Raymond was already swearing. White hair and red face. A drinker. But a genius. Paris VIII with Deleuze, attended Derrida's lectures, taught by Vidal-Naquet.

Then translated Deleuze.

Then, probably because of a highly nervous disposition, he had ended up in this dump. The swearing took on a mantra-like form.

Raymond had been asked to wear a name badge last year for the first meeting with the new Dean of School.

He had sworn like this then, in the staff office, sat in the same chair. Then he had emerged at the meeting with no badge. The Dean had asked his name and then she had asked why he wasn't wearing his badge.

'I'm wearing it,' he said.

'It's on my underpants.'

And so began a new special relationship.

The spirit of 1968 had never received its full satirical send-up, but here it was, swearing.

Philly went about with flappy dismissive *yeah yeah* hand gestures.

She negotiated the institution via its semi-conscious track marks, its scents, its olfactory trails, its rumours and personal lives. Whose husband she was going to connive into her bed next in order to push away for another few weeks whatever invisible mental stigma her upper class family had branded her with, to make her hungry.

To make her psychically, vampirically, backstabbingly hungry.

For this is how empires are maintained.

She did not deal with official emails or letters unless their function was as a personal projectile; darts to be thrown at others, or darts that were thrown at her.

But the darts travelled through the air slowly, giving her time to suggest to the right people—without of course ever actually saying it—what might happen to their faces if it hit hers.

She left to go to her studio, where her illustration students waited. Little versions of her with doll make up and doll dresses in the Right On Building, Angela Carter novels in their fishing bags.

The Right On Building. You couldn't make it up. You didn't need to. It had been called something very similar to 'Right On' and renamed when the art school took it over.

It was full of macrame hanging things. A wicker chair hung from the ceiling on a chain by the aloe vera plants which were climbing out of their pots they were so prolific.

Some of the macrame hanging things held spider plants that could've been called suffering, if spider plants could suffer.

Perhaps they could, the way things looked here gave no indication of their real state.

Others, others just hung, their purpose unclear. Grey heads of wild Glastonbury hair in offices.

The Email had not eaten them. It had not transformed them into suited and booted neoconservative wonks the moment it had been opened.

It did not need to. They were on their way out through generous retirement packages.

But even if they were to be in place for another two hundred years, they had slowly become something else over the last twenty or so.

Across decades of diplomatic immunity from everyday brutality.

They had become something abstracted that thought it was more concrete. Something that thought it was more even-dealing, yet operated with a high-handedness that verged on tyranny.

And this morning that something actually talked to the other somethings.

Today they could be heard discussing ethics in the abstract.

Because of The Email.

He had to get right out of earshot. He edged past them and continued down the corridor to his seminar room.

He registered a feeling of dread. Atomised though this feeling was, it was being pumped from a very particular place. It hit the nervous system, causing a tangible tremens, a particle level perspiration, ambient nausea.

A mild ailment with no official diagnosis, but very specific causes.

Some of those specific causes loomed back up like ghosts because today he had tutorials with students. Here was one ghost.

The student in his tutorial who had dragged his lazy self back in from a skiing holiday and claimed a photo taken from inside the chalet, of water droplets on the window, was 'uncanny'.

He had explained to the student that if anything, the image was the opposite, it was homely.

The student hadn't understood the concept of the homely and unhomely in the uncanny. Nor, clearly, had the lecturer who had lectured it to the student's group. He had then re-explained its origins in Freud, in a tired voice, after a very long day.

The student, humiliated, left with a face like a smacked arse.

The student then complained officially. He had been reprimanded for not 'being encouraging'. A formal verbal warning was registered, which had now expired.

But from then on if a student turned up claiming their cliched abstract painting was 'sublime', that it inhabited—symbolically and aesthetically—an interzone between beauty and terror, and if they also claimed to have been inhabited by the spirit of a dead eighteenth century homosexual sailor as they made this edgework—this happened in 2017—he would simply grade it at an above average level citing 'clear engagement with core module theory'.

His entire philosophy was rooted in a Hegelianism of a sort which demanded total openness to one's own unfolding within history.

It was the Hegel of Marcuse's Reason and Revolution and Charles Taylor's book on Hegel and Modern Society.

He couldn't remain in post under the demands of the activities of that post and do justice to his philosophical life.

He was therefore becoming a problem to himself. He needed to see a doctor. He was a doctor, but he needed to see a doctor.

To his colleagues though, since the reprimand, he had become the solution.

His colleagues thought that he had been a pompous twat and now he was getting better.

To them, his failure was a success. His students no longer complained.

He had failed. They had failed. And that was the solution. Well done all.

Here, to fail is to succeed.

If the uncanny were to be found, or the terror in the everyday, it lay in meeting these individuals—staff and students alike—and in facing the fact that one actively, consciously, failed every day.

He beeped the door open with his staff card and went in. Estates staff had left some window blinds on the floor.

He couldn't guess if they were meant to be fixed up or taken down. In any case the screws were new and so he pocketed them.

Another expense he couldn't afford, dealt with. He had to mend his door frame as he had left his keys inside for the umpteenth time and had to shoulder it in.

He cleared the blinds to one side. He cleared away the empty card coffee cups and half empty crisp bags.

Humans. They could bring their shit in, but they could never manage to take the debris out.

He had spent a long time teaching Marx to try to pass it on. Now they turned up with strings of words, including 'ideological', hanging out of their mouths covered in slime. When they did, they induced sheer horror in some unfindable place within the stomach.

He didn't want it to be like this. It wasn't always like this. He had converted some well. Around two of his students every year left in a state of absolute epiphany. He had been doing it long enough to have found the ratio. These often became friends. But some years the absolute cream were a couple of stoned kids wandering around saying 'bourgeois' in their £200 trainers. He couldn't take it anymore.

The other staff were evangelists. Higher Education had been attacked mercilessly by the Tories and the coalition with the Liberal Democrats. The ground for this assault had been set by New Labour. He should be screaming blue murder along with the others. But when he saw the reports that directly attacked 'low value HE' he felt himself curl up with embarrassment over what he had seen here.

He needed to defend his colleagues and the university he worked in. The middle classes were re-scripting the game to keep the elite Elite. But he had lost his faith. Now he consciously, actively failed every day.

He had lost his faith because the Millbank riot halted nothing. He was at Millbank, but had to go home early to let the cat out. He had then gone to the pub and the pub TV blared an entirely constructed helicopter view of hell out to credulous millions. He knew then that everything was sewn-up forever.

He had lost his faith because he had realised that everyone was ridiculous, including himself. This realisation began with the atypical event of leaving a world-historical riot to let a cat out of a house. But afterwards, the realisation would not go away, it kept growing exponentially.

He had lost his faith because the man who called himself an anarchist had slashed the hourly paid workers with no consultation and had got away without even a single complaint, because he had placed himself on the union committee.

He had lost his faith because the union committee, therefore, was corrupt.

He had lost his faith because a colleague defended the man who called himself an anarchist aggressively to him, and then defended the corrupt union committee.

The colleague did this only a few weeks after slagging the man who called himself an anarchist off to him via email. He occasionally looked at the emails and messages, just to pinch himself.

He had lost his faith because it turned out that this colleague had benefited from the hourage cuts the man who called himself an anarchist had made.

He had lost his faith because he then discovered this same colleague hired one of his former students to teach for no pay despite talking the socialist talk. Yet the weird abstract universal evangelism just kept on coming out of him, and out of most of his colleagues, on social media.

But his crows saw everything. They saw everything and they told him everything they saw.

He had lost his faith because here they taught existential depth like they were showing them how to sew on buttons.

To have faith, in this place, demonstrated a total lack of faith.

Losing your faith, in all this, *was faith.*

He went into the corridor and into the empty lecture theatre opposite. He scanned under the seats in the lecture theatre for coins. Nothing. The change machine in Fallowfield Sainsbury appeared and then evaporated in his inner space.

He passed the tiny kitchen next to Anthropology.

He pocketed a fistful of teabags. It helped him get through on the wage, but this had all gone much further. His resentment was starting to course through petty theft like a virus in the bloodstream.

Recent hauls included a ball of string and a kettle (PAT tested).

In the Cockroft Building a cluster of sofas backed onto bookshelves. These were filled with novels, volumes of poetry and academic texts on a wide array of humanities and arts subjects.

He went back across the corridor into the seminar room. He pulled the empty rucksack out of his satchel.

He switched on the PC. It booted up. He entered his username and password. He pressed the usual button on the desktop console to force the PC to connect to the projector hanging from the ceiling.

Nothing happened. He clicked restart.

He went to his bag and retrieved his notebook. He leafed through some of the scribbled ideas. Eventually the PC was back up. Still no connection to the projector. He opened his PowerPoint slides.

He planned to go through essay writing, referencing and critical thinking with his students today.

The last round of essay submissions had been beyond poor, but of course, they passed. He couldn't show them on the PC screen as it was backed up tight to the wall in this tiny room. Why there was even a projector in here was beyond his understanding.

He switched the PowerPoint to 'view slideshow'.

Nothing appeared on screen. He keyed through the different modes on the console. This sometimes worked.

Still nothing.

He picked up the phone and dialed 365, the tone switched from the start of a dial to a continuous alarm, to a melodramatic hospital flatline.

He put the receiver down and tried again. Exactly the same thing happened. His instincts took him down the back of the phone, following its cable to the socket—all fine there—he followed its black, shiny, S&M aesthetic back up to the phone.

One of the inner wires was visible, but it seemed attached. He picked up the phone and dialed 365.

Again, the tone switched from a split second of dial buzz to a flat, high tone.

Staff could be found all over the building on their knees, trying to rewire something that a colleague had unwired in the previous session while trying to wire something.

The metaphorical potential of this image was not lost on him.

He wished it were. He knew there was no correlation whatever between the ability to wire up a computer and the ability to understand the intricacies of Adorno. But there it all was. He knew that exactly those sorts of arguments appeared on the cover of the Daily Express and Mail and corroded everything that was good, not just out in the wider world, but in his own working class family, and in his father.

All of the above whammed through the mind like a bullet train as the stupid meat fumpled about with the cable and the plug. No wonder he was permanently exhausted. No wonder he went home to sleep like the dead from the moment he got into his flat. No wonder. And so within so without.

The situation in here was the same as out there. The police worked on their hierarchy from sheer evil down to a plain annoying they never ever got to. The plain annoying—traffic offences, fist-fights, burglaries—all devolved to the citizen volunteers. They were so under siege, and the management were so incompetent, that record keeping had almost completely halted. The entire Weltgeist wanted rid of all those 'issues' so it could get on with its yacht bouncers and city hitmen, its gated enclaves and bomb-strutted cars.

In here, you had to improvise a favela IT job before you even got to the point where you tried to evacuate your decaying brain of all that it had learned across the last twenty-odd years. Sometimes you never made it.

And that pretend anarchist-manager made babyish comments about 'the pigs' in meetings before going back to his private residence. He couldn't take it anymore.

He had stopped asking why these people made it into the lucrative jobs a long time ago.

He now knew that the two things were positively connected, like a USB cable to a laptop.

High salary and position was connected to an ability to inhabit the sheer paradox of several incompatible philosophies at once. In short, to talk utter nonsense at full volume one hundred miles an hour and never make it to the final revelation of the complex of paradoxes they called a 'self' that would cause the necessary total breakdown of the organism.

He wished the total breakdown of the organism upon them all.

He went out again. As he went up the corridor and back past the Profs he caught another earful of them. One of them had just said 'ethically problemaaaaatic' in that Glasto drawl.

He wished he could vomit it back up, out of his mind, or back out through his ears, or to blast it out at them like the verbal fart it was. Waste gas.

He reached the office, the fire door was propped open. Bloody Philly. She was up and on him before he had time to move past her and to his corner of the room.

He didn't have a desk, only a place where he put his stuff.

'Old man can you have a look through this when you get a moment,' she started.

'Ah OK, print...' she said, almost dreamily.

But her body was in scramble mode to get the document never intended for his eyes, which had nothing to do with his responsibilities, onto pieces of innocent white paper, which she could then force upon him, in order to be rid of the whole thing, at least in terms of the alibi she could now give, that he was 'checking it over' for her, 'an extra pair of eyes yeah?'

He ignored the comment, squeezed past her and picked up the phone. Dialled 265. Swore, put the receiver down. Picked it up again, dialled 365.

The ring tone worked here, but it shifted every 30 seconds or so as it rang around different extensions. Nothing. He put it down and rang again. The office quietened as the printer stopped shunting paper out.

Silence. Philly put a fat wad of A4 in front of him.

He stared at its obscenity, incensed.

A validation document for her course.

He replaced the telephone receiver more gently than he had ever done in his life.

He did this because he was intensely aware that his default mode was to slam it down so hard that it might smash through the desk and then the desk through the concrete foundations of the building and the foundations of the building into the earth far enough that it might be covered over and something new might grow there, something not-human, something nothing to do with humans...

'Philly,' he picked the document up and rounded on her.

'Philly,' it seems strange that I have just happened to wander into this office—having avoided it for so long, I think we both know that—to be given this task. You were of course going to email me to ask me to do this right? You haven't—of course—just opportunistically thrown this off onto me?

Philly refused to look up from her email, 'you don't mind old man, yeah?' she coughed.

'I know it's a pain but... *another pair of eyes yeah?*'

He put the A4 document down on her keyboard as she sat with her arms hanging down at her sides, gazing at an email from a friend.

'Send it me as a Word document and I'll do it,' he said. She had to regain her posture to catch the fat wad of A4 before it slid off her keyboard, scattering all over the floor.

They both knew the Word document would never arrive—by email or any other method—because that would mean he could do one of two things.

These were, i) copy it into a plain text document, make some minor, sensible changes to the front ten pages of the document, then riddle the latter three quarters with awful obscenities and then paste it back into its original Word document, sans for-matting—send it back and say that it was now fine, or ii) send it to his line manager asking if this was his responsibility.

His line manager's fingers still showed burn marks from the last inappropriate workload allocation he had attempted to pretend was fair: so the man who called himself a communist would tell him to ignore the request and Philly knew full well that he would sabotage the document in digital form.

He knew that she knew, that he knew that she...

But despite this knowing, they did this. They did this in full knowledge, in a place that was supposed to be entirely engaged with the process of bringing different kinds of knowledge to light. New knowledges...

As the California wildfires ate up more miles, as the sea filled with plastic crap. As European towns that have been asleep for hundreds of years are washed clean away. As nuclear non-pro-liferation treaties were withdrawn, they did this.

What he needed to watch out for now was the curveball that she might serve him in return.

Luckily he hadn't fucked her in the car park like Mike had, at her invitation, after the end-of-show party. She had Mike by the balls. By the balls.

Only then did he notice that Dan was in the corner.

He sat in the corner repeating 'you are joking me' and 'page by page, page by page, page by page...'

Dan had lost it.

This term he had been spotted with a carrier bag full of books that turned out to be self help guides.

He had been written off by the doctor three times across the previous two years and much less specifically but more finally in the heads of his colleagues this semester.

He had bounced against the bullying line manager and to the doctors, then out of the building and then against his wife when the reduced payments kicked in and then back into the building... to the back-to-work interview and the phased return, then the full return and the end of term and straight back into a line manager now psychotic with stress.

To the doctors, then out the building and then against his wife... His head span. It span like a pinball.

It was so strange that he couldn't see these cycles. His colleagues saw these cycles clearly, just not the pulsing dark energy propelling them from underneath.

They could not see this. They were exhausted from covering his teaching for no extra pay, only a vague verbal promise of time off in lieu which never arrived.

Nobody stepped in. Nobody stepped back to comment on the cycles that were gradually edging Dan to suicide.

Here, he thought, were humans. But here were humans who considered themselves to be radical, egalitarian, socialist, even communist. All the isms that had morphed to take the place of Christianity. Truly, the opium of the people.

But only these people. Because call centre managers didn't call themselves Mythogeographers in staff meetings in order to renounce the current quality audit.

He needed to leave. He needed to see a doctor.

One member of university staff held the opinion that non-conformism had shifted sideways into universities. But he never expressed this opinion to anyone.

Still, he had written some notes towards an eventual piece of writing on the matter with a small literature review.

What nobody knew was that Dan was being haunted by the ghost of a cat. A kitten, to be precise. He had also just been diagnosed with arthritis. But this was nothing. The kitten was behind it all. It had re-emerged. He had put a digital watch around its neck and set the alarm when he was a boy. He watched it leap in the air.

It had been affected for the rest of its life. Not trusting people. Defensive. Not wanting to be bothered. He had made its life sad. And now it was back to haunt him.

And he deserved it. He deserved it to return as a twelve foot high black feline to paw him to death. To play with him. The play he had denied it. Until his body was irrelevant strings of bloody muscle fibre and nerve.

The universe is evil. And he was part of it.

3h ago UK takes legal steps needed for European Parliament elections

3h ago Russia and Turkey will jointly patrol Syria's Idlib—Putin

3h ago UK government has not given Labour Party the undertakings it needs on Brexit—Corbyn

3h ago EU lawmakers back fines for internet firms that fail to remove extremist content

4.

A Shock, a painful loud sound. In the first few moments he doesn't know who he is. All he can see is a pattern of glowing lines. It's a whole second before his brain can tell the time from these shapes.

Four red digital numbers cut down the middle with a colon: 6:30. For now this is all there is in the universe, three numbers and a torturing, constant bleep.

At 6:32 his identity slowly begins to emerge, along with the full extent of his hangover.

He's Tod Male and he isn't grateful. He switches on the light. He takes off the black suit he went to bed in and yawns. He overstretches and pulls something in his shoulder. More pain. He switches on the ancient television and a beach slowly fades into view as the cathode warms to its task, filling his vision, overtaking him, thankfully.

A family runs down the beach hand in hand, teeth gleaming. The camera focuses impossibly on one of the digitally airbrushed smiles, a voice is saying something...

'TOD!' Len shouts up the stairs. 'We 'ave to gerrit all started, come on now.'

Tod stares numbly for five more minutes at the television before pulling on his green work corduroys, picking some scabs of dried paint off them with his thumbnail.

He grabs a check shirt from the wardrobe and walks down the stairs. Len has already gone out, so he pours some cereal, looking at the cockerel crowing on the box.

It looks like some kind of vision or nightmare.

A human-cockerel cross-breed in front of a cartoon red and orange sunrise like a kamikaze pilot's bandana.

'That's no cock arve ever sin,' thinks Tod, out loud.

This is the first time he's seen the cereal box. Mum used to leave it in a Tupperware container with a large serving spoon inside, on the rigidly enforced understanding that everyone in the house was only ever allowed one scoop per day.

Then Tod realises and smiles. There'll be no more of that nonsense now, the cereal box stays proudly on the table. Tod is free.

With the funeral out of the way he can do what he always wanted to. Both his parents are gone and he has nobody to please or disappoint. Today is the day he's been waiting for years to come, for half his life. He suddenly feels a twitch of guilt for thinking this, but the feeling of sheer release overwhelms him again just as suddenly and stays there.

He finishes his cornflakes and luxuriates in another half bowl, gleefully feeling like he has just broken one of the ten commandments. He sets off to work, the knowledge that he can now carry out his plans glows inside him like emotional Ready Brek.

He walks across the filthy yard, a few bantams cluck around his safety boots. He goes into a large corrugated iron building, which looks incongruously new compared with the rest of the farm, which is old and in need of repair.

Len is at the doorway waiting, with the usual blank look in his eyes, slowly chewing something.

'Mornin' Len,' says Tod.

'Tod,' Len replies matter of factly, his name a full stop as much as an acknowledgement.

They move inside and Tod's eyes adjust to the gloom created by the insufficient strip lights. Len shuffles around moving empty boxes in a seemingly random way. He turns to Tod.

'I'm in a stew are you?'

'What?' Tod replies.

'Stew Tod, stew.'

'I don't understand,' Tod protests, but Len cuts him off.

'I started boxing thaa clucks over thee-urr as they're t'noisiest.'

Finally, something he can respond to:

'Oh, right you are Len... I'll start with these over 'ere.'

Len starts to stack the boxes he has already filled.

'In a stew, soup stew,' he repeats.

*2h ago Brazil minister says he will shrink, not replace environ-
mental agency*

*2h ago Russia signals OPEC and allies could raise oil output
from June*

*2h ago Nationalist EU parties plan to join forces after May elec-
tions*

*2h ago Government sets out plan to comply with Brexit delay
law, if it passes*

2h ago French anti-meat activists jailed for vandalising butchers

5.

He could hear her before he could see her.

He turned the corner into the office and when he could see her what he saw was louder than just the shrill noise echoing down the corridor.

Orange headscarf, zebra-striped earrings and some sort of 1980s playsuit in turquoise. On her screen, 'Decolonising the University, by Philly Hamilton-Farey'.

'Philly's hanging out here today,' Vicky explained, knowing exactly how much he hated her.

Philly had told him last year at that horrific party that her father had advised on The Navy's new HMS Juffair base at Mina Salman, Bahrain. He had looked into it later. The Bahrain human rights record had been described as 'dismal'.

The Navy were bound up in slaving, from 1660 when Charles II founded Royal Adventures into Africa, a company set up specifically for overseas plunder. Then later, after abolition, the Navy had been tasked with closing down the slave ships.

And then that weird dream last night. The chicken factory he used to work in down the valley where he was brought up. Why did all of that have to resurface now?

Still, it was shaping into the bare bones of a pretty screwed-up short story.

One which needed to go straight in the bin.

And here she was, with that accent. Braying, whinnying, slicing. As self-aware as a floorboard.

After all of that. After the seventeenth and eighteenth centuries.

'Looked over that document old man?' she asked, with a snide look.

Licensed and naturalised murder, rape, torture and slavery. After the colonial breakup with its wars, mutinies and bloody revolutions.

After the commonwealth subjects moved to the centre of the fragmenting Empire for a better life, only to find racist abuse and more bloody murder, to find themselves refused by landlords, in cinemas, in pubs, in nightclubs, in hairdressers, here she was, our saviour.

Not only saving the university from itself, but saving herself in the process. An autopoetic redemption machine with a first class degree from the Royal College of Art and an MA with Distinction.

Two years ago, when he started, she had been wearing what looked like felt riding trousers. He had asked her about them. They were part of a Nazi uniform. She had got them off eBay.

Now she repeated the word 'Gilroy' over and over again until it sounded like the squawk of a parrot.

'Gil roy gil roygil...'

She even looked like a parrot.

He had never seen her at a union meeting.

Why the fuck did she have to be in here today?

He remembered the VC's speech the week before. A public school educated white man in an elite role smoothly outlining pronouns as *he/him*. 'The culture wars': None of it presented even the slightest kink in the VC's game.

Here, decolonisation was immediately being colonised.

He opened his iPhone. Looked at his feeds. Methane dunes discovered on Pluto.

He was obsessed with this stuff. There was an image of the methane dunes with the piece, from the journal Nature.

Frozen particles blasted by a wind that scientists had thought too weak to do so.

It looked like the desert, or sand dunes on the coast, only rendered in the chrome grey of the imaging technology.

But there was a realness about the picture, even if it was a giant frozen fart, it was the universe, and it seemed more real than any of the meaningless nonsense he had to tolerate every day.

He read Nature like schoolboys kept top shelf magazines under their beds, although he guessed that nowadays their pornography would be online.

He had come to the conclusion that there were no more great humanities academics. None. Perhaps Imogen Tyler. Or Saskia Sassen. But she was near-scientist. OK, no, there were a few.

Philly switched from her new crusade of decolonising the university single-handedly to an anecdote about one of her trips to Ascot. Something about people fucking on car bonnets. Vicky was laughing.

Pluto was only discovered in 1930. Two seconds ago, in the grand scheme of things. And I have to listen to this?

I want to be out of here. I want to be out of her.

He left. He sat in the cafe. He has been writing science fiction, partly influenced by his reading of Nature and New Scientist.

He opened his latest story synopsis on his laptop.

Inside him a cold lake drowned itself in a dead ocean.

6.

Len muttered whilst he worked as any other person might whistle. Tod had become used to his constant nonsense language over the years. He had learned to shut it out in the same way someone who lived by a railway line would eventually stop hearing the sound of the trains.

Tod makes a start on a new batch of chickens.

He felt he was putting on an act for Len this morning, going through the motions in order to make good his escape.

Because he was acutely aware of this, he hoped Len didn't notice he was acting strangely, and think something was wrong. Hopefully Len would put any change of mood down to grief—or his hangover—but Tod felt absolute elation, and kept catching himself grinning.

Tod comforted himself with the fact that Len was almost totally backwards and wouldn't have the sensibility to pick up on Tod's lack of grief. If he diagnosed his mood at all, Len would think Tod was happy to be the new boss of the family business. But he never wanted to inherit the farm, he was never interested in the work or the isolated life.

Taking four chickens at a time by the feet and dropping them into boxes, Tod made good progress. Though he disliked this kind of farming he was pleased with the new regulations for the transportation of live poultry. It was much more humane, the chickens were carried in roomy cardboard boxes with a couple of air holes in them. The boxes were cheap and could be recycled.

He dropped four more chickens into a box, they scrabbled to right themselves. After some initial noise the lid was shut on them and they were silent. This way they didn't realise their fate until the last split second, if at all.

Their memories were so short they probably felt as if they'd had a lifetime between eating their last feed and being slaughtered. None of them ever grew old enough to lay eggs. Their place in the pen would be refilled by identical chickens the day after they were gone, waiting there until they were ready to go to the slaughterhouse themselves.

They were making excellent progress and just as Tod was thinking of suggesting an early lunch, he turned to get another box and nearly jumped out of his skin.

Len is standing about an inch away from his face. The sight of his long nose, greasy greying long hair and spots at such close quarters was enough to turn Tod's stomach...

'Gonna get some feed. Ah need me brain food, ah need me brain food...'

Tod looks at his watch, it was ten past twelve.

'Oh... alright Len. I'll finish these and follow you up.'

Tod watches Len walk out of the shed and up to the house.

Len lodged at the farm in a little outbuilding. His bread and board were part of the deal. He got rations.

Tod had often thought about this. He got rations too, he supposed. But that was different. His parents had run the farm, he lived with them and stood to inherit it.

Tod always thought that if he was in Len's place he would have lived in Morden and driven up to work each day, but Len had always been part of the farm, ever since Tod could remember.

Thinking of him outside of it just didn't seem to work somehow.

Still, dwelling on how Len was tied to the place made him think about his own predicament. Len would probably want to inherit the farm instead of him if he could, but then he always knew his place somehow, he had never seemed ambitious. He just muttered his way through.

Tod's ambition, however, was about to be realised. In the past he'd always deferred his pleasure in the present moment for this day, in the same way as both his parents had waited for a retirement that never arrived.

Len mutters to himself and slurps his chicken soup, dribbling most of it down his chin. A car horn sounds in the yard. He goes to the window, rests his bowl on the stone ledge and peers out to see a driver from Murray waiting by his van to pick up the boxes for the slaughterhouse. Len leaves his soup and goes out to meet him. The driver's a regular and asks where Tod is. Len sees that Tod's car isn't in the yard.

'Probly darn at yewer place, they an't bin payin' up proply...'

'They don't bloody pay anyone properly mate,' the driver replies. 'Oh well, if I don't see him when I get down there tell him I'm sorry,' he adds.

Len stares blankly at the driver, the only movement coming from his slow chewing.

'I mean, about his parents like?'

The driver sighs at the dormant Len, wishing he hadn't tried to get into a conversation with him, and after an uncomfortable length of time Len replies, 'arr...'

He turns and starts to rummage in a box for an invoice. The driver carries the last of the boxes to the van. 'Fuck me they're 'eavy'.'

Len follows him out, pulling an empty trolley. He gives the driver the invoice and looks at him with his head tilted to one side then says, 'why buy chickens when you can buy an apple and some walnuts?'

The driver snatches the invoice impatiently out of Len's hand and gets back into his van.

He always dreads this stop, especially if Tod isn't around.

The van turns in at the industrial estate. Perfectly identical corrugated iron lock-ups like mini hangars stretch all the way up to the vanishing point. The van pulls up at one of them, the sign outside reads 'Fowl Smells' and underneath, 'poultry butchers and purveyors of fine cooked meats since 1985.'

Inside, Desmond puts boxes through the machine. He watches them go down the conveyor belt and into the dark holding tank.

Here the boxes automatically upend, the chickens drop swiftly down a steel chute to a razor which takes their heads clean off. No pain, little mess.

The next stage is a grim one. A special drill takes out the chicken's innards via their rear ends, but Desmond knows it's silly to think that this is unpleasant because, of course, the bird was dead by then.

Next, they are automatically plucked, their feet removed, washed, wings tucked, before going along to the ovens where they are coated in a solution made from a brown powder. This is a colouring and flavouring agent, in which the chickens are steamed.

Finally, they are chopped, sauced and put into ironic 'Fowl Smells' foil packaging and sold as meal-for-one deals in supermarkets.

Since the MD changed the company name sales had trebled. In a saturated market they stuck out like a sore thumb and the punters seemed to appreciate the joke.

They voted with their money. Good thing too, Desmond was up for a promotion soon.

The whole automated system was now run by just seven operators at different points down the line, whereas last year, before total automation there were fifteen. Desmond knew that some of their money would soon be coming his way. He was about to get his share and about time too. He had kept his head down. The ones who complained and joined unions had already been let go.

He'd be the supervisor of a system that pretty much ran itself. Easy Life. Not to mention the extra cash. He'd be able to impress the birds with a spare bit of that in the Cross Keys. He'd be a fanny magnet in no time. There had been some bitching about his promotion as rumours got out.

Desmond didn't care though. He knew what he wanted. Big fish eat little fish, it was the natural order of things. He knew what side his bread was buttered on, if the others didn't want to get into the race then they should stay out or stop complaining. Big fish eat little fish all the way.

Suddenly, there is a loud commotion further down the chute. Desmond runs and opens the inspection hatch to see a chicken has gone down the wrong way and has had its feet removed instead of its head.

He grabs the thrashing bird by the neck and runs over to the table with it. He picks up the cleaver and raises it. Carefully making sure his fingers are well out of the way, he brings the heavy cleaver down on the chicken's neck.

This happened, but rarely. It didn't worry Desmond, it was just part of the job and had to be done. It was big fish eat little fish again, the natural order of things.

Desmond was a carnivore through and through. He hated the sound of the whining vegans and vegetarians he heard on Sunday lunchtimes in the Cross Keys, moaning about the selection on the menu. Pathetic. Not to mention unnatural. Lefties and queers.

Tod thinks. Crouched in the dark his mind feels clear and he is sure the decision he has taken so long to arrive at is the right one. His escape is now so near he can hardly wait. He is adamant that he will leave the past forever, forget completely the truth he daren't even admit to himself.

The past is now a vague series of impressions, tastes, colours, and in this vague wash one or two specific things drift, mainly trivia.

Getting lost on Blackpool Beach then being found again by his father.

Eating apples from the tree in the yard that was now a withered stick. Occasionally a dark memory bobbed to the surface and he tried to make his mind swim elsewhere. Walking into the tractor shed to find his older sister.

The investigations that ended nowhere, accusing eyes on him every time he ventured into Morden. His father had grieved himself to death, his mother followed soon after, telling him on her deathbed that the loss of his sister didn't matter because they had needed a man to carry on the work at the farm after they were gone, not a woman.

He had hated her for those words. Tod's family had to be left behind, because, despite all that he'd been through, despite how his life with them had warped him, he still knew right from wrong.

Len walks back up to the farm. No sign of Tod, he's late back. He goes into the outbuilding and gets into bed fully clothed. He sets his alarm for 4:30 and starts to drift off.

He salivates, feels himself falling, wakes to catch himself. He finally falls and is running through trees naked. Tod is there too, running with him. Big bare-breasted Amazon women run after them. One catches Len, throws him to the floor and sits on him. Tod runs into the trees. She puts a crossbow to his head, starts jabbering something he doesn't understand. Len screams for release—into a lot of sickness—jabbering him-her he he—hideous glimpses

…this bit is really terrible…

eyes, hormone, but now he grows conscious thoughts jungle memory power naked faded growing pain and constantly salivating outside, receding, splitting, mother bolt phagocytosis voice loves, screaming with pierced use, he sucks the catch…

…so bad…

Spent, she puts a bolt in his head and cuts his throat. He feels the hideous pain fading, at the same rate as he sees his own blood seep into the forest soil and undergrowth.

He blacks out. When he wakes he is no longer seeing through his own eyes. His dying body transferred his very being into her when the bolt was shot. It feels like he's being born backwards, like the film of a birth played backward as she sucks him in. All that's left of him is inside her now, splitting.

…absolutely dreadful. Fucking Burroughs. But sort-of funny as well…

He can think, but her thoughts confuse and mingle with his, telling him to be quiet and to do as he's told. His inner voice is constantly silenced by her inner voice. 'I'm in a stew,' he tells her, but she doesn't listen, she shuts him up with her superior mind power which clamps down on his being like a vice, silencing him. Sometimes he gets glimpses, pictures of the world outside through her eyes. Hunting, killing, sickness and rituals. He's growing in her belly but he's not fully Len anymore, not even half Len, his identity receding all the time, until it becomes a faded memory. He can feel the pain of phagocytosis as her Amazon cells ingest his. He's a foreign particle integrated, but more like pressganged, into their community. Only part-conscious, like a phantom pregnancy. He can feel her hormone imbalance like bad weather in the distance. He grows. She feels the weight as she carries him and resents his presence. He's coming out now, the light is so painful, like the buried memory of the arrow that pierced his skull, a point of freezing ice-light, he goes into it screaming... screaming... He loves mother, they go out and hunt for men, catch them, sit on them, take their seeds...

…how old am I? Twelve?

Jesus Christ. I am so depressed.

I can't even write any more...

Len wakes sharply, sits up, sweating with wired alertness. The alarm goes off precisely in tandem with the one built into his body clock. Numbly he gets out of bed and starts to mutter. 'Instructions, instructions.' He opens a large drawer which reveals a grid of batteries. Row upon row of identical cylinders all with the same logo facing neatly upwards. He takes out two and puts them into a torch. He opens the drawer below it which is full of shotgun cartridges, all in similar rows. He takes out a handful and puts them in his coat pocket. He puts two in a double-barrel shotgun which he keeps propped by the bed. He fixes the torch to the shotgun barrel with black electrical tape, turns it on and goes out into the dark muttering, 'instructions, instructions, instructions.'

1h ago Boeing's 737 production cut hits its shares and those of suppliers

1h ago In call with PM May, Ireland's Varadkar says open to Brexit delay

7.

He walks out of the university. He was becoming a walking cliche.

He had been writing a novel with no plot.

Work. On the surface it was all worthy rhetoric. Underneath it was as warped as any other institution.

Management. A network had essentially taken it over, an unconscious masonic cluster operating through middle class yahing.

The quangosocial, the mutual noshing-off sessions, the in-flated incidence of people describing their profession as 'artist' on passport applications.

The Zukinonanism. The methane centre ballooning out, in the seminar room. The dreadful 'art'.

It all made him want to chew his own knees off.

And the book. He had the detail, but not the shape. The description of how it was. But perhaps there was really only the detail of how it was...

He got home. Went into the kitchen. He pulled open the freezer drawer. Frozen ties? Then he remembered.

The moths. The moths had been eating his knitted vintage wool ties. He was trying to save the last of them by freezing the eggs out.

Sometimes, it was like he was stalking himself.

Some days he ran back to philosophers such as G.E. Moore, away from the usual Kant, Locke, Hume and Hegel.

Because he forgot so much of himself in the daily chaos,

because he was so occupied by those he had to deal with to get by, he only re-inhabited some aspects of himself when he re-encountered them, and because of this he knew for certain that a world 'out there' beyond his sense existed. G.E. Moore thought it existed fine and that the sceptics were nuts.

In some odd way the more he lost himself the more he was found.

It was just that when he found himself again he discovered a walking cliche.

He had been writing a novel with no plot.

He had been freezing his ties.

But Joyce and Beckett no longer fitted. The times were neither fantastical nor oppressive enough where he lived, but...

He had been reading. Zygmunt Bauman described how Walter Benjamin categorises, at one point, stories as either the peasant tale or the sailor story. The peasant tale is cyclical and connected to the seasons, whereas the sailor's tale is exotic, bizarre and stretches credulity. They are the stories of the locally-rooted and of the explorer.

But Bauman thinks the two categories of story have fallen into one another due to our globalised, hyperconnected social world. Bauman wrote of his urge to present 'sailor stories as told by peasants.'

Inspired by all of this, he needed to write a book in which it was hard to tell where the sailor's tale ended and the story of the peasant began.

But for something to have coherence in the sense of a world, everything has to be consistent, even the things that are invisible.

He was so tired. Nothing could be done right now.

8.

Desmond works methodically, the boxes are slid four at a time out of the van rear and onto the conveyor belt. He sets up another load and goes for a break.

He goes into the canteen for a cup of coffee. Luckily there's no-one around, all the other workers have gone home. Desmond is the only one doing overtime.

He takes the latest copy of Club out of his bag and starts to flick through the pages, thinking smugly about how he's now on double pay for doing this. When he's the supervisor he'll have his own office and won't have to rub shoulders with the other plebs at all.

He is suddenly filled with confidence and the cosy feeling of privilege, this was it now, all the way up forever. Once he learned how to keep the books and get the orders he'd set up on his own, then he'd be happy. He tilts the magazine ninety degrees and cocks his head, looks down at the centrefold, his view slightly spoiled by the gash of the page split.

When he's made a pile, birds like these'll be begging for it, forming a queue. He drifts into a reverie; he's lying on a four poster bed, thirty identical blondes wearing only stockings and suspenders are lined up outside his mansion in the country, in the Lake District, no, in Wiltshire and

YEAAAAAAAAAAAAAAR

The scream seems to be atomising every particle in the atmosphere, it seems to be filling every sense, electrocuting his nerves...

He nearly falls off his chair.

It cuts off as suddenly as it started, leaving a silent, negative space in the air.

He drops the magazine and runs out of the canteen. He races to the inspection hatch and opens it.

Inside, theatrically framed, is a pair of human feet chopped off at the ankles in their shoes and socks, spitting blood and twitching to an inaudible rhythm, possibly a bossa nova.

He runs down the line and opens another hatch to see a man bent double minus his feet, the bloody stumps leaking all over the conveyor belt. His fat rump is in the air. Desmond slams shut the hatch, covers his head and winces just before the drill goes in and another hideous scream numbs everything around him. There's a smell of musty, burning corduroy.

Desmond walks back to the inspection hatch and picks out the feet which are now completely still. He walks over the shop floor with them at arm's length, carrying them with his little finger daintily outstretched and nose wrinkled, as though the severed feet smelled bad, which they didn't.

He walks up to one of three large brown boxes in a little-used corner of the building by broken machine parts and greasy tools.

He lifts out the box marked 'Suicidal Farmers' in large stencil lettering and then drops the feet into it. He gets his coat, clocks out and leaves the building.

9.

He had a hundred things to do. Marking, prep. He had to register for that bloody conference. He felt like doing none of it.

He thought about his pet theory, that they were all in an interregnum between classical and quantum physics, between an industrial modern world and the AI future. Of course quantum theory had been around for some time, but he was convinced the social world always lagged behind by a good fifty years. They were also in the very last days of the world as a single seamless *scape.* From now on, large parts of it would become the land of no-man. It would be the quantum world, but a world with *corners* again. What was the point of marking and prep, in the face of that understanding?

He went back to his feeds. He knew that what he saw on the screen wasn't the thing being described. The methane cloud was as good as a photograph, but a recent revelation regarding three 'super earths' had been a nest of representational problems.

What was being shown in the media was flux data that then gets transcribed into—essentially—illustrations. The illustrations made him fully understand how amazing it is that humans had found the objects in the first place, and they were there alright.

As though he had discovered woodlice wearing shoes, and those wood lice could read his mind. He thought about Kant.

But recently he had got to the point where he began to wonder if he were only himself, or all the humans in the world, those living now and those that had ever been.

The final mystery, why am I only me and not everyone?

He needed...

Why hadn't he made an appointment with a doctor?

He felt like he was being flooded, drowned from the inside out, the water rose in him and spilled out of every orifice, all that had been solid was becoming liquid.

On his screen the Carl Larsen Ice Shelf. Larsen himself died running a whaling factory. The crack down the middle of it caused by the discoverer.

Its naming becomes its end, once it has a handle it is as good as gone. Larsen whaled the whales almost to extinction.

Maybe we were all everyone until we gave things names.

Maybe the naming itself began the process, the destruction of everything.

He watched the video of the Carl Larsen Ice Shelf. But he had to go soon. A severe weather warning was in place all over the country. The rain hammered into the grass outside. It came down like stair-rods on everyone.

A student sat on the opposite table. He had a strange haircut, it was shaved up the back and long at the front. He was wearing a t-shirt with scorpions on it.

He turned back to his writing. Another half hour. Notes for a possible sci-fi novel.

We open this chapter in the northern quarter, in Manchester, which is now a walled ghetto. We focus in on a Land Rover safari which drives through this now semi-derelict, sleazy space, entered and exited by personal papers, checked by the military.

Many are permanently imprisoned here, never allowed out. In-debted hipsters are identified by a binocular-holding man stood with his legal team, in one of the Land Rovers, in a pith helmet. Hipsters run for cover, screaming with pure terror, some are netted, some are shot. He has bought, at great cost, a licence to do this from the local authorities. There is a bullet-proof glass car trailing behind the Land Rovers full of wives and mistresses drinking champagne, wearing highly decorated, baroque-looking clothes and jackets. They are taunting and ridiculing the inhabitants of what has been renamed by the fascist state, the N4R Ghetto.

Via conversations in the glass car and on the street, switching between the two—and the two social perspectives—we are told that the N1R Ghetto is what used to be Longsight, but it stretches right to the edge of Stockport.

It is ghetto No.1 because of its racial mix and proximity to Chorlton, which is now the centre of the city, the seat of local Christian government, because the town hall was bombed by Islamic extremists, during the civil war:

N1R is particularly brutalised and under extreme surveillance. The N2R ghetto is vast, but less intensely policed, it comprises most of the poor areas of north east Manchester, from Failsworth through to Middleton and beyond, whereas the northwest of the city is now all affluent, and gated off, from Media City to Prestwich. N3R is mythical, the stuff of rumours. It eventually turns out that it is an underground extermination, torture and interrogation bunker. N3R is Room 101.

We return to the action, two hipsters have their arms cut off and cauterised, in full view of the other N4R ghetto dwellers. A woman with particularly elaborate hair is scalped, and her earlobe extensions amputated. There is now a trade in the 'full sleeve' tattoo arms of hipsters. In England, in 2073, the neo-Fascist government has outlawed the tattoo, but the remaining examples have become highly prized, at the same time as the hipster livelihoods have been vastly reduced, as has everyone's, except that of the elite.

The full sleeve arms are skinned, preserved, treated, and used for boots and coats of human leather for the super rich elites. The Westminster neo-fascist dictator wives wear them, as do the media moguls of their propaganda wing.

Some poor hipsters have their arms amputated and new ones sewn in, for money, to pay their way. There are back room 'surgeries' in the N4R ghetto for this to take place.

The replacement limbs come from people even lower down the social hierarchy, who have sold theirs.

Muslims are particularly segregated in 2033 and some hipsters end up with dark-skinned arms, these are social stigmatic signs, for which they wear long sleeves, and the long sleeved come under suspicion. So, the short sleeve T-shirt and vest are again, flashy items of social status. Because they show that you've got 'naturals'. The caste system of the 'arm' is in effect. These back street operations often don't work, and people can be seen with gangrenous and withered limbs, walking around the N4R ghetto.

He begins to think that he should have social snobbery towards people with leather jackets made from leg, rather than full sleeve arm tattoos, in this story, in exactly the same way as we have snobbery over different cuts of meat. In and around this, a girl tries to survive and in doing so acts as a key narrator. He was struggling with her. He was struggling with her as a character.

It all needed work. It all needed a bin.

But no. It needed its own characters to carry out some violent re-ordering of their own story from within. He needed them to then continue outwards and murderously restructure all of the myths surrounding him. It would not be difficult, most of the myths were empty husks, which the wind could blow away.

He left the university and went to the Asian supermarket across the road.

He counted out silver coins for a three-for-a-pound cans of chopped tomatoes deal. Last month it had been four for a pound. The old lady in front of him was even worse off than he was.

Her coat had mould spores on it, but over two trillion pounds were on the island. Some of it moving around, flowing through deals and exchanges in which there were clear winners and losers.

Much of it, though, was frozen, as he counted out silver and copper. More of it, in recent years, flowed offshore.

Here, in Manchester, Real Holdings salted it away like new imperialists. Like the old East India Company they managed themselves through a deliberately mind-warping set of nesting umbrella businesses. Russian doll capitalism.

'I hate those Russian dolls,' he told himself his favourite joke in his head, 'they're so full of themselves.'

He unlocked his bicycle, stashing the cans in the precarious bike basket made out of a green plastic vegetable box.

Cars on pavements. So-called Smart Cars in between cars, sideways and pedestrians also squeezing themselves sideways through the remaining cracks.

Two trillion. Fifty pound notes stacked in piles the size of sub-urban detached houses in a warehouse the size of Reading city centre. Grotesque Domestic Product.

But it was never stacked there, only in facile Guardian articles and misleading A Level exam papers that were supposed to pre-pare young people for 'real life' was it ever stacked anywhere, even theoretically.

Although the quantity was sort-of right, if you were prepared to give or take many hundred millions.

And nobody had ever managed to redistribute it or defy its logic.

Nobody had managed to give or take any hundred millions.

None of the monarchy, politicians of the left or right, citizens, Conservatives, Libertarians, Fascists, Mutualists, Feminists, Existentialists, Liberals, Anarchists, Xenophobes, Buddhists, Pacifists, Christians, Marxists, Terfs, Trans, Neomodernists, Postmodernists, Vegans, Vegetarians, Islamists, Postcolonialists, Nihilists, Greens, Sikhs, Queers, Deconstructionists, Post-in-dustrial men and especially the wooly-thinking supposedly apo-litical everywoman and man had ever managed to do anything fundamental about it. And nor would they.

The best anyone had ever managed was a minor adjustment. A major achievement in this world, right enough.

But most minor adjustments meant nothing to the poor and everything to the rich. Most minor adjustments went unnoticed by the masses as they silently tipped what was a small fortune to them into the bank accounts of the most feral, smug humans on the planet.

As he cycled through the cycle lanes that seemed to have been designed to kill as many cyclists as possible, swerving to avoid the Range Rover with blacked out windows—a Darth Vader helmet cruising slow—the icecaps melted, a dripping that was becoming a flood, coming down on him now, on his coat with the safety pin holding the right arm on, on the bicycle held together with clip-ties and rubber bands.

Philly rang in his head like a hangover, 'sustainability, sustainability, sustainability...'

Nobody was sustainable, but everyone had entered into a world in which—to seance Orwell—nobody is sustainable but large swathes of humanity are far less sustainable than the others.

He had told her this. She had told him that he was 'so negative'.

That was all it took for these people to rule the rest.

An ability to convince others that to jolly up and jolly well pull your socks up was a state of nature and not a massive con trick linked to a vast Ponzi scheme.

If you were 'so negative' you were a dangerous crackpot. This rhetoric was more explosive than to call someone a traitor.

Because it came across as reasonable, commonsense, a fact, to the idiots that made up most of the country.

England had sucked this up and the Tories were in forever, therefore, in these last days, it was the End of the World.

But no help was offered to the dangerous crackpots. They could get madder and iller as they worked for the moneyed. Psychoanalysts were not offered to these crazies. If you murdered people you got analysts. But not if you were simply sick.

Not in Britain. But actually, to be precise, in England.

Wales was more civilized. Scotland was more civilised. Scotland was probably going to sever itself from the mess. Wales was refusing to build any more new roads forever, as England was planning 5,000 more miles of them. Ireland had essentially gone to war on England and so as far as he was concerned, it was more civilised.

Some of them had been Marxists and so much the better.

Negation. The only true form of thought for the modern holy person.

Phone notes

Your eyes are never fully open but to keep them fully closed because of that is not a game to get into evidence they are never fully oh open when people say she looks like a Fiona or Lightning is a great name for a cat you can get them more half oh open so you can see and analyse but you have to shut them ex times in ex hours and lose control over the images your brain projects, yet on waking still act as though this is an aberrance that hasn't quite yet been corrected in some ways you can see and analyse better through the lids, that letter box of half open slits receives mail but you don't know what's in the envelope.

But you still think that there is something in there, not yet understanding that the envelope is the letter do you half dream you can see through your eyelids between waking and sleep, I do... the brand new ideas of Sigmund Freud or at least they are to Johann Hari… they may as well be to every fucking one else who gives Ted Talks Ted Talks are given by institutional bullies and arseholes but dressed in their envelopes all button down flat white comforting undercut buzzword mouth full of greased ball bearings.

Disturb Your Certainties really is a good name for a cat.

Can we at least agree that between the arse cheeks there is a hole for shitting out of and that men have tits the only use for which is pleasure...

1h ago 'Why in God's name?'—Irish, British leaders mourn murdered Northern Irish journalist

1h ago Scotland will prepare for a second independence vote regardless of UK—Sturgeon

1h ago Islamic State video throws spotlight on suspected ringleader of Sri Lanka bombings

1h ago Biogen dips as strategy post Alzheimer's setback fails to impress

1h ago Result of 2014 Scottish independence vote should be respected—May's spokesman

1h ago Iran's Zarif warns U.S. of 'consequences' over oil sanctions, Strait of Hormuz

10.

Desmond drives over the moor road and slows down to almost a stop at a particular place. The Smiths' 'That Joke isn't Funny Anymore' comes on the radio and he turns it up slightly. It reminds him of certain birds at school. Tara. And Gemma Fielden. Fucking tits on her. His car stalls. 'Shit.' He winds the window down, thinking that at least he'll be able to hear better with the engine off.

He comes here every night. Sometimes he only slows down before driving home, sometimes he stays for over an hour.

A car is parked in the layby and is gently rocking. The light is on inside but the windows are steamed up. An occasional squeal can be heard. Desmond tries to see inside, but it's just too cloudy. He unzips his work pants.

Suddenly a cold object touches his forehead and his heart leaps. He twists in his seat to be blinded by a glaring light at the end of a double barrel shotgun, which is right up against his face.

'Oh god, oh god I'm sorry, I'll go, am I trespassing? Is that it? I'll just go...'

'Get thee out thaa car perv.' A voice orders.

There is something in the voice that Desmond knows isn't quite human, something he instinctively recognises and pan-ics.

'Look mate,' he forces a smile, 'I'm sure we can work this out, I've got money...'

'Get thee out thaa car,' the now livid voice repeats. Desmond gets out.

A spotty old man with lank grey hair down to his shoulders is sighting him down the barrel, one eye wide and one shut.

'Up tut farm perv.'

'Oh please, take my car if you want,' begs Desmond, struggling to disguise the rising hysteria swelling in him.

His hands are shaking, he wants to run but can't.

'Shut it. Or tha'll be nourishment for't worms. Chicken feed my lad.'

Desmond walks, pushed by Len's gun barrel, up the path towards the lights of a farmhouse in the distance. He holds his hands up and out to the sides as if about to be frisked against an invisible wall.

A tiny voice within him, almost totally drowned out by panic and adrenalin realises that the man hasn't told him to put his arms up, but he is doing it because he's seen it so many times before in films, and it suddenly feels like he has gone through a million forgotten rehearsals for an event that is now nothing but physical, livid panic.

The voice is washed away by sheer terror, an inner force which powers a wide awake need for practical escape. But he knows if he runs he will die.

They reach the farmhouse.

The man directs Desmond to a bare room just off from the kitchen. He is told to face the wall. He faces the wall. His mind desperately probes the situation for the slightest chink of light, when might it be possible to run, when should he chance it? Suddenly there's a sharp blow to the back of Desmond's head.

Desmond wakes up on the floor with a violent headache.

He can hear muttering from the other side of the door. He can hardly move with discomfort. The temptation to pass out again is nearly impossible to resist, but he knows he can't allow himself to submit to it. He lays a while longer hoping the pain will subside, but it doesn't, so he tries to move, making a mental inventory of pain, arm damaged, numb, could be bad, blood on face, blind fucking head pain.

He drags himself the short distance to the door and props himself up on one arm, the straining tendons and muscles joining in with the horrible music coming from his inbuilt choir of biological alarm bells. He puts his eye to the key-hole. The man is pacing, rabidly talking to himself.

Chickenortheegg, chickenortheegg, chickenorthe...

The man suddenly stops, like he has remembered something important, and rushes to a telephone in an adjoining room.

He picks it up and dials. He dials 3-6-5.

As soon as he starts talking, Desmond pushes down on the door handle and finds it unlocked.

He pulls himself up onto his feet and creeps out into the kitchen in a crouched position, praying the man won't turn around, trying to be noiseless with a clumsy twisted foot and throbbing headache more unpleasant than his worst ever hangover.

He makes it across the kitchen floor without alerting the man and manages to open the front door just enough to slip out.

Once outside he sets off running down the path as fast as

his foot will allow, but the wind is strong, it's like pushing against an invisible wall.

He runs past a large, modern corrugated iron building and an engine starts up behind him.

He looks back to see the man emerging at an incredibly slow pace on a green John Deere tractor, its exposed wiring sparking at the sides. Desmond runs behind the building and the wind drops a little. He puts on a sprint but it's no good, the air seems condensed and he's running in slow motion down the hill. The tractor engine is getting louder and louder.

Desmond keeps looking back, trying to push against the invisible aspic which seems to have suddenly formed in the air. The tractor can't be going one mile an hour, but it keeps up. Running is like swimming through treacle now.

Desmond's muscles ache from the exertion and he feels he will pass out at any second. He sees the main road and his own car, which now has its bonnet up. Wires are trailing out all over the sides. Desmond starts to sob as he pushes on. The other car is still in the layby though, and the light is on. Thank Christ. Desmond heads for it screaming for help. The tractor is still gaining.

He rips open the car door and the shock suddenly stops his shouting, he stands panting and inside there's a couple alright, but they must be almost seventy years old. One is in the passenger seat nearest to Desmond, he wears brown swimming trunks with a brown belt and a gold clasp and holds a severed chicken's foot up to his mouth.

He's pulling the tendons at the bottom, making the claw mime to his words, which he speaks in a mocking helium voice:

'I'm sorry, we can't help you at present, I'm sorry, we can't help you at present, we are busy, we are busy, I'm sorry, we...'

The woman is in the back seat, wearing a bikini.

She's pregnant and appears to be going through contractions. Her waters have broken all over the leather seat and there's a smell like warm chicken soup, a slight feverish steam in the air, the source of which is not obvious. She has a string of sweets on a necklace which she bites into with each contraction, she moans, squeals and squirms with the pain.

Desmond feels another blow to the back of his head and he goes down. He passes out less immediately than before, staring up at the old man's chicken foot puppet twitching over the edge of the car seat.

He is glad to go under this time.

He comes to, in leg irons which are chained to a big metal Aga cooker in the kitchen of the farmhouse. The man is pointing his gun at him from a facing armchair. The torch is off and the only light comes from the purple glow of the insectocutor on the wall which fizzes occasionally. Next to him, on a table are piles and piles of 'Fowl Smells' foil cartons, the lids removed, all steaming hot.

'Graze' the man says with a dead-eyed look, a passionless mask-face which makes him look as if only his body is really present in the room, as though he's being controlled by someone else, someone in another country who watches the scene through his eyes.

'Oh god, just let me go,' Desmond pleads, his voice trailing into a barely audible sob. The man puts the gun to one side and crawls over to him on all fours. He takes down a foil carton and opens it.

He starts talking into the carton; 'Tod, I miss your mam too, but we can't have you running away, no, noo, nooo.'

He's crooning now, making little cuckoo noises in the back of his throat.

He starts singing, *'she were a sister and a lover and a cook...'*

A tear is forming in his left eye which begins to slowly roll down his acne-littered face, like a moon buggy negotiating a series of craters. He pulls a fork out of his coat pocket and scoops some chicken towards Desmond's mouth.

But they 'ad to go, the moos ot cows spoke to me and ah could 'ear the message behind it with me 'ead, but not with me mind like...

The man pushes the fork into Desmond's pursed lips.

Desmond keeps them tight for a split second but is too scared to refuse.

The man pushes the fork into Desmond's pursed lips.

He swallows and shouts, 'You're insane.' The man laughs and carries on feeding him, talking into the carton as he piles food onto the fork.

Desmond spits some onto the floor and the man becomes angry and starts shouting: 'I brought you into this world and you'll not escape it as soon as arm 'ere.

AA'LL 'AVV ME A HEE-URR!

Desmond eats the whole container quickly and the man pulls another down. If he can keep him stalled by eating then someone might drive past, notice the car and investigate, there might still be a chance he'll get out of this.

The second mouthful is chewy and tough and Desmond can't swallow it.

He spits it out onto the floor and sees a piece of tattered, blood-stained green corduroy. His whole body suddenly vacates its current mode of being, it changes in a split second from fear, pain and discomfort to a state where every cell in his body is livid with total horror, it rises and rises until he can't breathe. He gasps frantically for air, half choking on chicken pieces.

He passes out again.

He wakes to the man forcing food into his already full mouth. This time he has a knife to his throat.

A shifting floor and numb feet. A light feeling in a heavy body, so light that it communicates how dangerous the feeling is.

Desmond eats the food he's given, sobbing weakly now, begging for mercy much less often as it does no good—the man only laughs and feeds him more. The soup from the dinners covers his face, it dries in his hair to form matted clumps.

The light feeling becomes normal. He knows that if he doesn't resist it, it might turn into pleasure.

Occasionally, a bit of bone or clothing is removed from one of the foil cartons as the man fills another forkful.

Desmond tries to vomit but he can't. The horror that previously filled his stomach, arms and legs is slowly turning into a numb pit, an empty, limitless space which seems to be waiting to be filled by something else.

Desmond welcomes anything but what he is going through. He keeps passing out and the man tries to slap him awake every time he sees him drifting out of consciousness. He screams and threatens. Desmond considers it a triumph when he passes into oblivion and occasionally catches himself going under with a feeble smile.

He's been eating for hours now, yet he doesn't feel full.

In fact he only feels more hungry. His mind is beginning to feel blank and he keeps forgetting what is happening to him. He welcomes the blackouts now.

He tries to remember how he got here but he can't, it's all just a series of delirious, unrelated events that keep changing every time he tries to list them.

Which came first? The chicken or the... car?

No that isn't right. Desmond stops trying to work it out. The food doesn't feel to be going just into his stomach now, it feels to be going down his legs, stuffing up his arms and going into his head, making him feel thick and heavy. He feels giddy and keeps passing out laughing.

When he wakes up for the third time he has a strange feeling that he knows where things are in the kitchen. For instance, in the sideboard by the Aga he thinks there is a set of teatowels, green stripes on orange cloth. A little later he's astonished to see the man open the door and take one out to mop his face for him.

Hours later, Desmond swallows the last forkful of chicken dinner the man has. He grins triumphantly and passes out.

11.

Work done.

Now he had to negotiate The Corridor on his bicycle.

The Corridor was rectilinear, horizontal, straight.

Horilinear.

It had no start or end. Nobody ever completed a pass through. You always found yourself in the middle. It was only cyclical in the sense that the particle collider at CERN was cyclical. You winked out here and immediately found yourself in it again.

Like the stuff CERN was finding, Manchester was no longer real as we know it. Manchester had been entirely swallowed by it own myths.

He began to push down the cycle lane. Pedestrians stepped in front of him, into the lane, gazing into mobile phones.

On good days he made sarcastic comments; 'try it under a car, it's quicker and probably less painful.'

Today he screamed profanities at them.

Some of them saw you, and then stepped out anyway.

'It's only a bicycle.'

And lo, the particles did collide here.

It was apposite that John Cockroft trod this corridor, inventor of the early particle smashers that led to nuclear power, nuclear bombs...

The Horilinear Corridor, the Horridor, was a different dimension entirely. Its spatial and temporal qualities were far removed from ours.

He had cracked ribs and a shattered knee from the last smash. He couldn't afford the buses and anyway they were so slow. The train company had discontinued most services to town from his local stop.

Whoosh. He found himself here, ribs healed, thrown back into the cyclotron.

The Corridor was now fully made-over. It even had its own website.

The Corridor Website told you that here is Where Emmeline First Began To Disclaim.

There are all the Pankhursts, but obviously it misses the bit about Christabel's mad, Second Coming of Christ brag.

The Corridor. Where innovative vegetarian business thrives, connecting to its roots in nineteenth century liberalism.

Where Rutherford worked on atomic physics.

Where Noel brought his first guitar.

Where Wittgenstein wandered.

Where he saw that bloke take a shit in that doorway at 1am who was not even homeless, just another early-30s coked-up pisshead far too far gone to care.

Our vision for The Corridor is Manchester's cosmopolitan, world-class, international quality, Innovation Park, where talented people from the city and world work, create, socialise, learn, live and do business, contributing to the economic and social dynamism of one of Europe's leading urbozones.

The word 'world' signified nothing at all and everything at once.

Skinny jeans round knees squeezing one out, with a look half of pleasure, half of having vacated his brains along with his bowels.

A sound behind him spiked his nerves. A guy was panting 'coming through mate coming through.'

There wasn't enough room to come through.

Somehow the other cyclist overtook, millimetres away. His ludicrous lemon yellow lycra shorts and Italian cycling cap shrank in front of him. Lycraman was dust.

But he was dripping with sweat. His shirt soaked and cold.

An Innovation Park is where agencies communicate with each other via action potential events and transmitters, where razor-edge institutions, hubs and companies connect with start-ups, incubators and accelerators. Compact, transit-accessible, technically-wired, Innovation Parks foster open collaboration, grow talent and mixed-use housing, offices and retail.

A car fired at his left side, pulled up to the junction and stopped so hard there that he jammed the brakes on, swerved and spat.

The spit hit the bonnet of the white BMW, the owner shouted CUNT out of the window. It was all done in seconds. He pressed on, listening for the screech of revenge. None came. It settled down.

The Corridor connects to the city centre and to surrounding neighbourhoods and so while embracing the distinctive qualities of an Innovation District we create a Sense of Place through placemaking and it is crucial that this crowning is investitured through collaboration and community engagement.

The junction loomed at the top end of The Corridor. A lot of cyclists seemed to be waiting on a green.

From impulse to act, the signal to satellite leap occurs in a nano-second, but in that nanosecond the signal passes straight through the noise of a hundred hyperaccelerated years.

Up ahead, a flash of lemon yellow, crimson and black. Lycra-man was scattered all over the junction. Lycraman was goo.

The Corridor.

Where the fifth Pan-African Congress was held.

Where John Robb buys organic food.

Where the first Civic University was opened.

Where Alan Turing created the basis for modern computing.

Where that giant dog toilet was discovered by a few remaining council workers, which led to the RSPCA and Police being called to evidence of dog fighting and suspected man-and-dog fights.

The past vomited itself back up again here, nothing ever went away. Even the deleted phone numbers of former lovers flashed up in neon blue from The Cloud to haunt you. Here, in The Corridor, it was harder to wipe it all out than to preserve it. This was the permahorror of the horrorlinear horridor.

Where, really, they worked out some of the key elements that led to the grim deaths of over 150,000 Japanese people. And possibly the end of all humans, some time in the future.

But here they all are, the Japanese, re-appearing out of the district in which the International Anthony Burgess Centre is housed. As though Burgess himself had re-opened that particular Stargate.

And look, there's Lycraman, he is replaced instantly and whooosh.

For Dividuals in Neoplace New Enclosures employ Nous and Algo to increase future-perfect Instrumentalities. Clene Kraftemes promote New Enclosures' vertiswell, including for-dynamis, movement and Bouff. The New Enclosure concept is Wilbeawl and is being refined with Gauges. Gauges are used to help with tapping-up how spliced Neoplaces function and contribute to define a New Enclosure.

The Whitworth. Where the arts elite nosh each other off and are condescending to the staff. In the restaurant that overlooks Whitworth Park. Swanning about in those expensive clothes they wear.

Whitworth Park. Wear, wear, wear. Where the horrifyingly violent sexual offense took place. Where that other thing happened as well. The horrorline horridor.

Put differently, one day we all woke up, there were no Starlings left and everyone was An Individual and An American who speaks American English.

You, me. Even the Chinese.

12.

He opens his eyes. In the first few moments he doesn't know who he is. He sees four red digital numbers cut down the middle with a colon: 6:29. The digits change to 6:30 and the alarm goes off. Suddenly there's shouting from downstairs:

'AAAAAMOS!'

'Yeah, I'll be right there Len,' he shouts back... yet feels slightly odd doing so. He can't work out why. He feels a massive bowel movement coming, but can't go. There's a tingling in his legs and arms.

'AAAAAMOS!' Len shouts again.

'What?' He replies.

'The police are here.'

Curious, Tod dresses and goes downstairs. A policeman and woman are waiting in the kitchen. Len is muttering quietly under his breath. The policewoman is looking at Len with thinly disguised disgust.

Their eyes fall on Tod. They seem relieved to find someone a little more ordinary looking.

'Sorry to trouble you sir, but we believe you were at Fowl Smells Limited yesterday.'

Tod tries to think but really can't remember what he did the day before. He notices the Emmerdale calendar by the Aga.

Saturday. Then he remembers.

'I do usually go over on Fridays, yes... I usually go to get the cheque and drop off the new invoice.'

'You didn't talk to a Desmond Greenwood did you sir?'

A stirring of deja vu rises, tickling his senses, but it is slight and vanishes as quickly as it came.

'I don't remember doing, no...' his voice trails off and his mind goes blank.

The policeman looks at the policewoman with a mocking face on seeing how confused Tod is.

'This man doesn't know anything,' he thinks, 'we've got a right pair of country retards here'.

'Well if you do see or hear anything of him please call us, he left Fowl Smells last night but didn't return home. His mother reported him missing. He was last seen driving up this way and through the pass by someone he works with, but he didn't come out at the other end. I'm sure he'll turn up though.'

Tod felt a pang of recognition, something about a car... but it was gone.

'Are you alright sir?' the policewoman steps into his line of vision.

Tod was lost in a trance, trying to remember something he had already forgotten.

'Sorry, what were you saying?' he asks, coming to.

'He didn't come out the other end sir,' the policeman repeated, as if to a child with learning difficulties.

'Yes, erm, I heard you. Sorry, I'm still a little tired.'

'Well if you do hear anything...' the policeman and woman move towards the door.

'Oh yes. Yes, you'll be the first to know,' smiles Tod, seeing them out.

He closes the door and goes back into the kitchen.

'Time for breakfast,' Len smiles, horribly, pulling the lid off a tupperware container of cornflakes and carefully measuring a scoopful into Tod's bowl.

That was most of it. He'd have to fill out the text later. He had filled in the more indeterminate gaps as he had written it up, but at least he had the bare bones down.

It was almost a full short story. It had fallen straight out of his head in a dream and then into his laptop the morning after.

'I have thought it my duty to my fellow-men to place on record these forewarnings,' he typed at the top.

12m ago Euro falls on weak German business morale, stocks slip

15m ago Trump says he is holding big Pharma accountable in opioid fight

17m ago Deep sea mining boss says new law could be adopted next year

Phone notes

The work hangover.

That story, coming back the other way, on a random week night, in New Street Station with colleagues, after that talk at that bloody gallery.

I totally agree with you on this, it is a divided country, class, ethnicity, generational.

But just how much locally-specific do you need with your water, sanitation, food, shelter, clothing, medical services, transport, jobs, education?

Now the flip into the competition, now we're all unsustainable, but more sustainable than next door.

Provincial, administered corrupt moralised. I don't know what re-localising power or locally-specific means, I don't think you do either.

The future is oh Jesus really? back to the nineteenth century and the history of early welfare Then it becomes an anti-capitalist thing, by localising do you mean removing global finance from the picture? if so it's a false chase.

This rich hippie claiming she's a peasant, everyone unsustainable, but some are, some are much more than others.

What's missing in all this is uncertainty and you can't put uncertainty back into certainty like that without ever mentioning it.

The local is created everywhere by the global and vice versa, why is community always *cutchy*. Community can be brutal. Community is closer to the sociology of a bunch of secondary school kids in a playground. What is this sudden glowing figure the peasant offered like a bucolic vision of the shepherd, in bible stories, or the classical idyll? Berger got harder the older he got, but by far too black and white, his peasant romanticism isn't something...

Do you really want to make everything? bread, butter, shoes, houses, when would you do your art then, artist, or is that an un-alienating step too far?

Global finance rips things to shreds, but I still don't get this...

Do you know how much time it takes to harvest the seed from ten sunflowers? Half a day…

I don't understand why I was invited to host this talk at all, I turned it down once but they insisted...

It is really just a bit silly, localism isn't a box of stuff you can open and apply to a town...

Do a sickie, vomit in the bin, no use, fingers... If I just leave them to it and nod a lot and make *mmm* noises maybe nobody will notice, maybe...

We're at the locally lost of Gradgrind... It rags backwards, the global Brexit But We then do the sixth and win with a Britain fantasy clearance, choose here...

Did he really paraphrase Orwell, or even an Ecover ad...

I'd rather you used 'indigenous', at least then I can hit you really hard...

13.

He gets off his bike. Walks the rest of the way home pushing it. Past the grammar schools and then the high rises. He processes and sifts some of the writing he's done.

He starts to stitch together a theoretical feminist critique of his last short story.

It seethed with castration terror. He slips into the jets of theory easily, in his head, while walking.

The Freud that he would need to underpin this critique—should he write it—the disavowal of Freud and Lacan from key feminists that would mark it out.

He hadn't had a television for fifteen years, not since he put the last one out—when he lived in Wales—after cutting its bastard plug off. Drink had been taken.

This kind of interior monologue had replaced TV. He thinks about how he might work an entire oppositional critique into the story he has been writing, but his mind wanders.

He thinks about how negative he has become. He thinks about his colleagues.

His colleague Jane was undertaking discourse analysis on celebrity magazines. Hers was one of the better research projects taking place in the university.

In fact, Jane was perhaps the only person in the university he would consider sane.

Last week she had shown him some copies of *Hello!* and *OK!*

It was a whole other world to him, in the way that the Financial Times colour supplement *How To Spend It* had shown him a whole other world.

But he knew that despite the worth of her project he could short-circuit it in a sentence.

He knew that *OK!* magazine means itself, it means *OK!* magazine. That *How To Spend It* supplement means *How To Spend It.* You only had to think of the outmoded term 'colour supplement' to access this level of reality.

The rich don't really do irony. The poor do. They have to, to psychically survive.

A piece of litter stuck onto the sky momentarily and then unpasted itself, it wafted like a dismissive hand gesture.

A few snowflakes fell in front of it. Grey-white at the back. The snow began to take instantly.

Come on wipe it all out this sadness like blind VHS crackle. Vertical hold wipes to horizontal hold wipes.

E. Smith knew.

E. Smith knew that a sudden covering of snow could tell you as much about the city you were in as an anthropologist. It showed it to you anew in a flash, like a revelation. It showed you its space, now abstracted from use.

The space means itself. The television means itself. iPad online means itself. All of psychogeography was this. This is why psychogeography remained what very excited people said about it and never got much further than what very excited people said about it... these days at least.

In a way it didn't need to. A sudden covering of snow showed the city to you anew in a flash, like a revelation. It showed you its space, now abstracted from use.

The snow fell. He walked automatically. He dodged oncoming clusters of people with complex movements without ever thinking about them consciously.

He switched back to the celebrity magazines.

But he was in the way. Jane was sane. Sane Jane. He wasn't.

He was in the way of himself.

He let himself fall into his symptoms. 'I inhabit my symptoms,' he once wrote. Then that bloody awful woman in his department had asked if she could 'borrow' the term.

Stupidly, he agreed. But what did Rotten once say? 'More fool you for only having one idea and that was somebody else's.'

He had limitless ideas. They fell out of his brain like snow out of the sky.

Some layer of his internal awareness patiently turned his thinking back again to the celebrity magazines.

Z-listers. One would hesitate to call them celebs, their nasal cavities becoming more cavitied, caving in to cocaine again and again.

The drug that whispers once inside you. That whispers that the fact that it is in you is just a coincidence and you just... you just feel great because you feel great and you feel great because you are great.

This is the only clearing in the postcapitalist schizoid chaos. But this clearing is hollow like the ruins of destroyed, fossilised lungs.

The only truth here is hollow. The truth is the inverse of this cokewhisper. That you are no-one, but you are only no-one because of the caving in to the cavity, cavernous, massive nulling of the world.

The most insidious drug for the most insidious society. People do work to do whores and whores do whoring to buy coke.

The social is in the condition of horrible slimy punters and prostitution. The most insidious social, in the condition of punters and coke whoring.

The social reduced to a surface of gleering advertisements for Z-list cokepunterwhoredom.

The spaces at the margins of the condition of Z-list cokepunterwhoredom are so narrow, so littered with the collaterals of Z-list cokepunterwhoredom that they are unliveable. Cold sweating hands pull you into the moil of Z-listers selling stories about other Z-listers to nothingpapers. Their facerot is nothing. Nothing compared to the murders over in cokeland where the coke is made. But still it goes on. They talk to the face in front. Face in front is always a new face each time they talk and it is always the same face.

And universities are this. And the art world is this and the literary scene is this and radical politics is this and philosophy is this TV is this every office is this every warehouse every workplace every shopping centre every high street and the…

That academic journal is becoming this. It is not there yet but. It is soaking up the white blot of cokepunterwhoredom. The clear serifs are vanishing.

Now it is just The White Blot.

All those greasy people on Facebook. Neowhite-town.

It is build a profile it is. It is becoming *OK!* and *The Star*. Because of cokepunterwhoredom. Try to resist caving in to the cavity, the Cavernous Nullworld.

But how? He fingers his staff card in his pocket.

Your passes, your lifeworld, spacejunk over Salford.

Suddenly a load of explosions. Fireworks.

3m ago

Fucking bonfire night, it isn't for another week... Ash and bits rained down ahead.

2m ago

Mancunians are fucking nutcases.

The trillion ton lake of black stars has taken the sky off, it will pour in on us all.

He reaches the end of Slade Lane and hits Levenshulme.

1m ago

In a nanosecond the sleet turned to hailstones like marbles.

Then needles fired from a trillion blowpipes.

Forthcoming at Erratum

bone bite snare - Michael Mc Aloran
Morant - Roy Goddard
The Prodigious Earth - Eric Blix

Printed in Great Britain
by Amazon